INSPIRE INCLUSION

Dr. Arpita Chatterjee

Ukiyoto Publishing

All global publishing rights are held by

Ukiyoto Publishing

Published in 2024

Content Copyright © Dr.Arpita Chatterjee

ISBN 9789362694454

All rights reserved.
No part of this publication may be reproduced, transmitted, or stored in a retrieval system, in any form by any means, electronic, mechanical, photocopying, recording or otherwise, without the prior permission of the publisher.

The moral rights of the author have been asserted.

This is a work of fiction. Names, characters, businesses, places, events, locales, and incidents are either the products of the author's imagination or used in a fictitious manner. Any resemblance to actual persons, living or dead, or actual events is purely coincidental.

This book is sold subject to the condition that it shall not by way of trade or otherwise, be lent, resold, hired out or otherwise circulated, without the publisher's prior consent, in any form of binding or cover other than that in which it is published.

www.ukiyoto.com

To Mother Motherland and Mother tongue

Contents

Preface	1
Inspire Inclusion	2
Sectors Need Inclusion	4
Investment In Women	6
Inclusion is not a one-day event	7
Areas of Inclusion	9
Pseudo Feminism	11
Trad Vs Mod Women	13
Womenpreneur	15
Government Schemes For Women	18
Quotes By Women ForWomen	21
About the Author	**22**

Preface

The world comes together to celebrate International Women's Day (IWD) on March 8th each year. The message of this year's theme, "Inspire Inclusion," is strong: we need to make a concerted effort to create a society in which women are not only visible but also fully included, respected, and empowered. Not only should we honor individual accomplishments, but we also need to acknowledge the amazing contributions made by women in all walks of life. It involves tearing down the structural obstacles that still prevent women from achieving their full potential, including gender-based abuse, inequitable pay, and restricted access to healthcare and education.

Inspire Inclusion

Inspire Inclusion encourages everyone to recognize the unique perspectives and contributions of women from all walks of life, including those from marginalized communities. One of the key pillars of Inspire Inclusion is the promotion of diversity in leadership and decision-making positions.

Leading and mentoring others: Stepping up, taking charge, and helping others find their path is also important. Spreading the word: Inclusion should be a no-brainer. Speaking out, championing diversity, and making sure everyone is part of the picture is required.His already prejudiced mind was far from the concept of inclusivity. Instead, he thought that the few of us women who dared to stick with the discipline and fight the odds would crumble under the pressure.
It feels impossible to try to move through what appears to be a solid wall. Ensuring that all individuals feel valued and encouraged, regardless of their identity, can often be equally difficult.

- Beti kamao- women in work force

- We as society when think of development and progress men and women have to contribute to it equally. When one half of the world's population is still fighting for equal opportunity and fairness then we need to collectively analyse where we are headed culturally. When we look at the figures of women in workforce it is very disheartening. Unless women actively contribute to the growth of the society economically it would be just a wishful thinking to have a fair world. Why even today we have to look for reservation for women in different sectors. Is reservation fair? Honestly speaking job should be based on merit and talents. There are some sectors where the presence of women is less or we can say they are not included. The question is doa woman aspire to compete with no? well the answer is a clear NO. We don't aspire to compete with men nor do we wish to replace them. Biologically men and women have distinct genetic, morphological and hormonal

characteristics that's something we need to accept and honour. It is actually beautiful and shows that the nature has intelligently designed the entire human race. By
- Let's see how that could be a possibility :-
- Encouraging the idea of women working
- Promoting women
- Conducive environment for women to work

Sectors Need Inclusion

Workplace

Ensuring that women receive equal compensation for equivalent labor and that they have equal opportunities to progress their careers through leadership positions and career advancements are two ways to achieve workplace inclusion. Fighting workplace discrimination, bullying, and harassment at work can put an end to unfair treatment.

Education

All women and girls should have access to high-quality education. They ought to have the same access to high-quality education as men. Ensuring proper inclusion and empowerment requires this. This entails dismantling current obstacles to education, such as biases, economic limitations, cultural norms, and violence against women.

Leadership and politics

More women need to be in the forefront of politics. More women must assume leadership roles and participate in decision-making processes in order to achieve inclusive governance and representation. Women's opinions must be fairly represented, and their voices must be heard. Women's political engagement must be promoted, obstacles to it must be removed, and leadership development assistance must be given.

Healthcare

Women should receive healthcare that acknowledges their particular health needs. Each and every woman deserves high-quality medical treatment tailored to her individual needs. This is crucial for inclusion as well as for their well-being. Inclusion can also be aided by avoiding prejudice in healthcare settings and by supporting gender-responsive healthcare policies and initiatives.

Media and representation

It is important to support women's representation in the media sector. More women will participate in the media if gender-sensitive reporting and storytelling are encouraged and prejudice in media content is avoided. The promotion of good roles and the image of women can be effectively achieved through the media. Inclusion is facilitated by the regular display of women's varied roles and accomplishments in the media. By sharing the experiences of women who have overcome obstacles and reached significant professional milestones, we may combat prejudice, gender bias, and stereotypes.

Innovation and technology

Women's participation and inclusion in technology can foster both innovation and economic empowerment. This can be accomplished through eliminating biases in technology design and development, encouraging women to start their own businesses, giving them equal chances in technology-related occupations, and encouraging their participation and leadership in science and technology sectors. Encouraging women to pursue careers in science and technology can help dispel the stereotypes that typically prevent them from advancing. Creating a world where everyone has equal opportunities regardless of their background, gender, identity, or socioeconomic standing is the goal of inclusion.

Investment In Women

There exist various options that can be pursued by countries, which are willing to invest in women, improve economic performance, and stabilise their growth trajectory. In this aspect, creating an enabling environment for women in education provides a good starting point. Providing women with the tools and chances to advance their economic and personal development, fulfillment, and empowerment is known as investing in women. This entails giving women access to forums where they may express themselves and effect change without compromising their autonomy and dignity, as well as training and financial support. Investing in women pays off in a big way. For instance, there is frequently a multiplier effect because women value providing their children with a quality education and sharing what they learn with their community. Since they are less likely to mishandle money, women foster trust. They are able to recognize and put into practice efficient solutions to societal problems due to their pivotal role in social dynamics. Furthermore, social cohesiveness originates from them. There are fewer disputes, less violence, and greater harmony when women hold positions of authority. By investing in women, we can make sure that no economic, health, or development opportunity excludes more than half of the world's population. Investing in women also translates into a generation that is wealthier, healthier, and more educated. Society as a whole gains from investing in women. The appropriate investments enable women to reach their full potential and give them the confidence to express their thoughts, discuss their opinions, and make significant decisions.

Inclusion is not a one-day event

It's an ongoing process that requires commitment and action from all of us. By working together, we can create a world where every woman feels included, valued, and empowered. Let's use International Women's Day as a springboard to make this vision a reality.

On this International Women's Day, let's all #InspireInclusion in the following ways:

Encourage change

Speak up against prejudice and gender bias in the community, at work, and online. Encourage groups that promote gender parity.

Dispel myths

Recognize your unconscious prejudices and actively combat preconceptions that restrict the opportunities available to women. Encourage varied and positive portrayals of women in the media and in daily life.

Encourage and enable

If you hold a leadership position, take an active role in mentoring and assisting women in developing their careers. Give women the chance to express their opinions and areas of expertise.

Make educational investments for girls.

The secret to enabling their achievement is education. Encourage programs that give girls access to high-quality education and give them the confidence to follow their aspirations.

Honor a variety of narratives

Honor and celebrate the accomplishments of women from many cultures, backgrounds, and spheres of life. We are all inspired by their stories.

Areas of Inclusion

For women to have a larger place at the table, inclusion is still required in a number of areas.

It might be challenging to be included at times.

Stereotypes

Biases and antiquated notions about what women and girls can and cannot do impede them. The expectations placed on women by society might prevent them from fully participating in a variety of settings by dictating specific roles or actions.

Obstacles in the system

Women may face obstacles to inclusion due to structural disparities in institutions, organizations, and systems. This can involve problems such as uneven remuneration, restricted opportunities for leadership roles, and a lack of encouragement for work-life harmony. Women may be prevented from achieving their goals by certain conventions and regulations. It's time to make things more equal.

Culture & Society

Customs and expectations can prevent women from pursuing their goals. This can include social conventions that elevate the views and perspectives of men over those of women, as well as cultural restrictions on women's autonomy and mobility.

Managing differences

Due to their color, origin, ethnicity, financial standing, disability, sexual orientation, and other factors, certain women have significant challenges.

Opposition to change

There may be difficulties in achieving efforts for gender equality and inclusion. Some folks might not be open to change. Attempts to question established gender norms or reallocate power and resources may encounter resistance from some individuals or groups.

Providing women with the tools and chances to advance their economic and personal development, fulfillment, and empowerment is known as investing in women.

Pseudo Feminism

Equality for men and women, as well as a level playing field that values the opinions of women, are central to feminism. Simply put, real equality. Since everything has two sides, everything has benefits and drawbacks. Feminism has no drawbacks, but contemporary women have an entirely incorrect understanding of it. In the name of feminism, they have started to demand everything. Feminists exist, followed by so-called pseudo feminists. The description of "pseudo-feminism" shouldn't anger a feminist like you. The tenet of feminism is that all people deserve respect, including women. It is pseudo-feminism that asserts that women are more deserving of respect or that individuals of different genders are undeserving of it. Some women enjoy cooking for their spouses, while others prioritize raising their children and taking care of the home over their careers. They are free to choose what they want to do; thus, this does not turn them into slaves. The worst statement is definitely "I will not cook because it is sexist!" and it's certainly fairly common amongst people who identify as fake feminists. Almost nobody on social media truly understands feminism, and those who do often adopt a pseudo-feminist persona. One of lady , who chastises the Roadies competitor who said he slapped his fiancée for allegedly cheating on him with five other guys, is another example of a fake feminist. She answer. "You're saying she dated five men? Listen to me—she made that decision."Perhaps you're the source of the issue. You do not have the right to smack someone. Additionally, she supported the girl by stating that it's her decision to cheat. You loudly demand equal pay, but you don't care that you have to make reservations to get into colleges. While we discuss shattering preconceptions, we make fun of a lady who chooses to be a housewife. Recognize that our physiologies and minds are wired differently, making us two different genders.Thus, give up automatically assigning blame to your gender each time your supervisor treats you less favorably than that guy coworker. It's possible that you are lacking something. Give up thinking that guys are misogynistic bigots and that the reason you fail at anything is because you're a woman every single time. Feminism is about recognizing that you are a woman with a palette of choices and that you should be allowed the freedom to make them. Stop disparaging this movement that drew upon the blood and sweat of hundreds of women in order for you to stand independently. I can choose to be a feminist even if I'm wearing pink and high heels. I have the option of becoming a housewife or serving as a front-line soldier.

Trad Vs Mod Women

The debate between modernity and traditionalism has been essential to our understanding of how traditional countries are modernizing. The majority of the time, modern was mistaken with Western. A sizable portion of Indian society likewise believed that everything Western was contemporary. Because Indian culture was the pinnacle of tradition, it was therefore hated for being superstitious, illogical, and lacking in reason. Fortunately, a lot of long-held customs and beliefs have recently received scientific validation. This pertains to Indian women as well as the entire Indian community. However, the argument between modern and tradition continues! These traditional women were discouraged from pursuing anything that may interfere with home life and were supposed to emphasize their responsibilities to their families in many traditional or conservative civilizations.

The family was supposed to be headed by men, while women were supposed to dress conservatively. In order to maintain the family, traditional women also assumed gender-specific responsibilities including childrearing, cleaning, and cooking.

Women in the modern era are free to pursue their own passions, objectives, and liberties. They have autonomous access to healthcare and education. They have the right to vote and represent the public interest when it comes to public policy. In addition to dressing and living more freely, the majority of modern women can pursue occupations both inside and outside the home to further their personal development.

Modern women have not been without controversy with the recent developments. When it comes to desirability, for instance, some men are attracted to women who used to uphold conventional values because of the assertiveness of feminists and the stability of the family.

Nonetheless, some men choose to share household chores while pursuing their separate occupations, or they align with the ideals promoted by progressive women and choose to take on homemaking and childrearing responsibilities. Today, there is usually space for both men and women to decide for themselves where they stand.

While expressing "why should I care for children is becoming trend among women these days," traditional ladies did not believe that raising children made them less than anyone. In the past, women were free to choose to become housewives or to proudly stay at home with their children. However, today's pseudo feminists are pressuring women to choose otherwise. When it comes to caring for their husbands' parents, most women now ask if they are maids, but when it comes to their own parents, they expect their husbands to treat them well. Traditionally, women did not distinguish between serving their own parents and their husbands' parents.
Conventional women attempted to lead regular, calm lives without attempting to rebel against society to demonstrate their feminist beliefs.
Although modern women believe wearing a miniskirt is essential to looking like an independent woman, traditional ladies did not wear them to demonstrate their freedom.
Cooking was not considered a lowly vocation by traditional women, but now days, so-called "independent" women make fun of women who cook.
While feminists would label you repressed if you said as much now, traditional women were not embarrassed to acknowledge that they loved their child beyond everything else.
While modern women believe disrespecting others is a sign of independence, traditional women understood the need of treating people with dignity. Men were viewed by traditional women as the other sex, not the bad sex.
While women today view marriage as a transaction where it's crucial to marry a wealthy and established man, traditional ladies saw it as a pure and lovely institution.
However, the majority of the younger generation—especially in metropolitan areas—adopts pseudofeminism; my response is focused on those women. Don't be insulted, please. Not all women are affected by this.

Womenpreneur

The process of starting a new business is called entrepreneurship, and it is creative and dynamic. An entrepreneur is a catalyst for change, creating jobs for others in the process. The process by which women locate possibilities, assemble resources, and set up a commercial endeavor in order to generate revenue is referred to as women's entrepreneurship. This entails applying abilities and knowledge to create novel goods or services, expand a clientele, and turn a profit. The entrepreneurship of women plays a significant role in propelling economic expansion and advancement by generating employment opportunities, fostering creativity, and enhancing societal welfare. The process of starting and running a firm with the intention of turning a profit is known as entrepreneurship. Historically, men have controlled the entrepreneurial world. However, women entrepreneurship has become more well-known all around the world in recent years. The process of starting and running a business enterprise by a woman or group of women is referred to as women entrepreneurship. Women entrepreneurs are driving economic growth, fostering innovation, and creating jobs, all of which have a substantial positive impact on the world economy. The many facets of women's entrepreneurship will be discussed in this essay, along with the difficulties they encounter, the advantages they enjoy, and the laws and initiatives that help them. A society's prevalent economic, social, religious, cultural, and psychological factors have a significant impact on the emergence of entrepreneurs within that culture. Women becoming entrepreneurs is a relatively new phenomena. A woman-owned business not only contributes to economic progress but also yields a number of positive effects.

Women Entrepreneurship in India

Indian Women Entrepreneurs
India is a land of business, with about 70% of the populace still working for themselves, with some estimates reaching as high as

80%. The idea of "women entrepreneurship" gained traction in India in the latter part of the 1980s and is now a worldwide phenomenon.

An entrepreneur is a person who can see opportunities in the market, gather resources, and put plans into action to launch and grow small, medium, or large-scale businesses. In India, the rise of women entrepreneurs and their impact on the economy are clearly apparent. Over the past ten years, women's entrepreneurship has gained recognition as a significant but underutilized source of economic growth. .In India, women constitute just 14% of entrepreneurs, overseeing 20% of micro, small and medium enterprises (MSMEs) among 58.5 million enterprises. This indicates that while women make up a smaller percentage of the workforce overall, they make up a larger number in rural areas, particularly in the entrepreneurship sector. Rural women who develop their entrepreneurial skills are better able to make decisions for themselves, their families, and society at large.

Challenges faced by women entrepreneurs

Women entrepreneurs encounter some distinct obstacles specific to their gender. Women entrepreneurs frequently encounter obstacles such as restricted access to capital and resources, discrimination based on gender, and juggling work and family obligations.

Limited access to funding and resources

One of the main issues facing female entrepreneurs is their limited ability to obtain resources and funding. Research has indicated that enterprises owned by women receive notably less funding than those controlled by men. There are several reasons for this, such as investor biases and the underrepresentation of women in venture capital firms.

Gender biases and discrimination

These issues present a significant barrier for female entrepreneurs. Research has indicated that female entrepreneurs frequently face discrimination based on their gender, including reduced income, restricted access to opportunities, and gender stereotypes.

Balancing business with family responsibilities

Women company owners frequently find it difficult to strike a balance between work and family obligations. Due to the fact that women are more likely to take on childcare duties for young children and aging family members, it may be challenging for them to dedicate time and resources to their enterprises.

Advantages of Women Entrepreneurship

Although women entrepreneurship presents certain difficulties, there are several advantages for female entrepreneurs. The development of jobs, innovation, economic growth, and more diversity in the corporate sector are a few of the biggest advantages.

Economic growth

By generating jobs and stimulating the economy, women entrepreneurs are significantly boosting the world economy. A survey by the Global Entrepreneurship Monitor states that almost 9 million people are employed by women entrepreneurs in the United States alone, who bring in $1.8 trillion annually.

Employment creation

Women entrepreneurs are also in charge of bringing about new employment in the economy.

Innovation

Women entrepreneurs are also driving innovation in the business world. Studies have shown that companies with more diverse leadership teams are more likely to be innovative and outperform their competitors.

Greater diversity

Finally, women entrepreneurship is promoting greater diversity in the business world. Women entrepreneurs bring unique perspectives and skills to the table, which can help to create more inclusive and diverse workplaces.

Government Schemes For Women

Today's women entrepreneurs have found success in pursuing less-traveled industries such as food, beauty, travel, sanitation, IT, automobiles, and even innovation. According to World Bank projections, if 50% of Indian women are employed, the country's GDP may increase by 1.5% points.

The Indian government has also taken action by launching lending programs specifically for women. These programs for women entrepreneurs will be very beneficial in helping them obtain the funding needed for their entrepreneurial endeavors.

Some of the popular government schemes for women to start a business in India are the Pradhan Mantri Mudra Yojana (PMMY), Bhartiya Mahila Bank Business Loan, Mahila Udyam Nidhi Yojana, Cent Kalyani Scheme, etc.

In recent years, women-owned businesses are scaling successfully, running side by side, and giving tough competition to even established household names. Yet, a recent Harvard study proves that women-run start-ups receive less venture capital funding as compared to men-led start-ups.

According to recent US data, women-owned businesses created a revenue of $263,091 in 2022. Despite this, women entrepreneurs often find it harder to get funding than their male counterparts.

But the good news is, several organizations in India are working towards providing assistance to female entrepreneurs. Some of the resources are-

Women Entrepreneurship Platform (WEP)

WEP was started by Niti Aayog, under the Government of India's initiative to support female entrepreneurs.

WEP aims towards sponsoring female entrepreneurs with benefits such as-

It provides funding and financial assistance.

There are many mentorship and skill training programs as well.

WEP also provides guidance in marketing.

It offers a community of like-minded talented entrepreneurs, to help budding leaders.

Mahila Udyam Nidhi Scheme

The Mahila Udyam Nidhi Scheme is a Punjab-originated initiative that helps small-scale industries by providing hassle-free loans.

The maximum loan amount under the MUNS scheme is Rs. 10 Lakhs, which can be availed by filling out a form at the participating Bank.

Udyogini Scheme

Udyogini Scheme is helpful to business owners with little or nothing, to begin with. The scheme provides loans to female entrepreneurs whose family income is less than Rs. 1.5 lakhs per annum.

Under this scheme, women who are widowed, destitute, or disabled can get a loan amount of Rs. 3 Lakhs at a low-interest rate.

While the scheme was started by the Karnataka State Women Development Corporation, several other banks have also adopted their own version of the Udyogini Scheme. To get a loan under this scheme, you can either visit the website or the bank branch nearest to you.

Dena Shakti Scheme

Dena Shakti Scheme is yet another option available to female entrepreneurs under the following sectors-

Retail Stores

Manufacturing

Education

Housing

Microcredit Organisation

Partnership firm business

If you are a female entrepreneur, who is trying to scale her business in one of the mentioned sectors, then you can apply for the Dena Shakti Scheme. This scheme will help you with a loan amount of up to Rs. 20 Lakhs, or it will depend on the sector you are trying to get a loan for. The base interest rate under the Dena Shakti Scheme starts at 0.25% and can be availed by filling out a form at the Dena Shakti Bank.

Bhartiya Mahila Bank Business Loan

If you are a woman trying to scale your business in the manufacturing sector, the Bharatiya Mahila Bank business loan can come of great assistance.

Under this scheme, female-owned businesses in the manufacturing sector can get a loan of up to Rs. 20 Crores, and if the loan amount is less than Rs. 1 crore, then there will be no collateral asked by the bank.

The scheme was first initiated in 2017, and even after Bhartiya Mahila Bank and State Bank of India became one, the scheme remained in place.

To apply for a loan under this scheme, you can either visit the nearest bank branch or call a representative at the registered number available on the website.

Our Prime Minister Shri Narendra Modiji taken initiatives to encourage women entrepreneurs and India soon will have 1.25 crores women entrepreneur.

Quotes By Women ForWomen

"Women are leaders everywhere you look — from the CEO who runs a Fortune 500 company to the housewife who raises her children and heads her household. Our country was built by strong women, and we will continue to break down walls and defy stereotypes."
— Nancy Pelosi

"Each time a woman stands up for herself, without knowing it possibly, without claiming it, she stands up for all women."
— Maya Angelou

"It's not about how many times you get rejected or fall down or are beaten up, it's about how many times you stand up and are brave and you keep on going."
— Lady Gaga

"There's something so special about a woman who dominates in a man's world. It takes a certain grace, strength, intelligence, fearlessness, and the nerve to never take no for an answer."
— Rihanna

"Women should be tough, tender, laugh as much as possible, and live long lives."
— Maya Angelou

About the Author

Dr.Arpita Chatterjee

Dr. Arpita Chatterjee is a homoeopathic doctor who owns and operates her own clinic, Healing Centre. She serves as the Head of the Department and an Associate Professor in the Department of Pathology and Microbiology at Parul University in Vadodara, Gujarat, India. Additionally, Dr. Chatterjee has been leading the "World Healing Society Foundation," an NGO dedicated to animal, human, and environmental welfare, for the past 10 years.

Dr. Chatterjee has been honored with several prestigious awards, including the Pride of Vadodara in 2019, the Chattarpati Shivaji Award in 2019, and the Women Achievers Award by Parul University in 2021. In 2022, her NGO received the Best NGO for Social

Awareness Award at the Constitution Club of India. This award was presented by the Honourable Speaker of the Delhi Assembly, Shri Ramniwas Goyal, from the National Achiever's Recognition Forum.

www.ingramcontent.com/pod-product-compliance
Lightning Source LLC
LaVergne TN
LVHW091536070526
838199LV00001B/96